PUFFIN BOOKS

Lizzy pink

Cherry Whytock lives in town with a big fluffy cat, a bouncy brown dog, her husband and one of her glamouroony grown-up daughters. She owns far too many clothes and has a rather large shoe collection (her favourites are sparkly silver with diamond ankle straps – YUM!). She likes sequins, bouncing her dog across the common, weeding her garden and making chocolate brownies.

Books by Cherry Whytock

FIZZY PINK

Fizzy Pink

CHERRY WHYTOCK

PUFFIN

for 🐔 Henny
With ♥

PUFFIN BOOKS

Pengu   Group ...   ...SA
Pengu   Group B2

Penguin Irel ...   ...oks Ltd)
Penguin G ...   ...stralia

P ...

Penguin Grou ...   ...Zealand

Penguin Bo ...   ...rg 2196,

Pengu ...   ...nd

First published 2005
2

Copyright © Cherry Whytock, 2005

All rights reserved

The moral right of the author/illustrator has been asserted

Set in 13/20.5pt Adobe Leawood
Made and printed in England by Clays Ltd, St Ives plc

British Library Cataloguing in Publication Data
A CIP catalogue record for this book is available from the British Library

ISBN 0–141–31901–1

Contents

1

Hello! It's Me!

My best friend, Pixie, has a pet snake. This is not the reason she's my best friend. The reason Pixie is my best friend is because I can tell her things and she listens.

Pixie was the first person I told when Mum and Dad said we were moving house.

'Fizzy, we're moving up in the world,' Mum said. I got worried that we might move too far up in the world and float off the top. Pixie said she didn't think that was what my mum meant. She was right. What Mum and Dad meant was that we were moving to a much bigger house on account of my dad having made loads of money decorating a huge posh stately home nearby. What they also meant was that we would be moving from our fantabby pink bungalow, two doors down from Pixie's house to somewhere FIFTY MILES AWAY, but they didn't tell me that straight away.

Pixie

The reason people call me 'Fizzy' is because my name is Felicity Amber Jade Pink. But honestly, I mean, who wants to be called 'Felicity'? Not me. As soon as I could, I told everyone that I would be called Fizzy. Now, even if someone shouts, 'Felicity, there's hot buttered toast and jammie dodgers for tea,' I don't even budge.

Apart from being called Fizzy, I'm nearly ten, and I've got loads of red curly hair and big fat freckles that sort of almost join together in the summer. And I can do backflips – sometimes.

I don't have a pet of my own like Pixie, but we do have a family dog. He's called 'Petal'. Petal is a bulldog and he is really brilliant at growling. I like him but not many other people do. I also have a baby brother. He's two and he's called Jack.

jammie dodgers

Sweetie Pie

Felicity Fizzy

Jack the Splat is what I call him because he splatters stuff everywhere. He especially likes splattering his mashed banana, but if he can't splatter that he will try and find the baby lotion or some of my dad's gloss paint to splosh about in. Jack's quite cool. Except when he splatters something disgusterous in my hair and Mum has to wash it out. GROTTYBAGS.

When Dad showed me on the map how far away we were moving, I went all wobbly. I mean, it didn't look like we were moving up in the world. It looked like we were moving left and down a bit. And it was *miles* and *miles* away from Pixie. I cried. I don't often cry because that's what babies do and there is no way that I, Fizzy Pink, would do anything that a baby does. Also crying makes my nose all hot and runny.

Mum and Dad tried to make me feel better. Mum said, 'I tell you what, Fizzy Freckles.' (That's what she calls me when she's being a bit soppy.) 'I've had a gorgeous idea. Why don't you and Pixie write to each other – you know, proper letters like people used to write all the time in the olden days? OOOOh, SO romantic . . . Tell you what, your dad and I will pay for the stamps. What do you think of that?'

What I thought was that most *normal* people would email each other, but obviously Pixie and I can't do that because:

a) Pixie isn't allowed to go online any more because she once stayed on for two days and nights by mistake.

b) Our computer doesn't work because my mum thought it would look nicer if it was pink, so my dad painted it and it all got sort of stuck together. CLEVER, I don't think.

But, on the other hand, when Pixie and I are old and fantabbymazingly famous we could make all the letters into a book and sell it for ZILLIONS of pounds. Maybe it's not such a bad idea after all.

2

And These Are My Mum and Dad

While Mum and Dad were packing up our house, Pixie and I practised writing letters to each other.

It took Mum ages and ages to pack up all her sewing stuff.

The reason Mum has loads of sewing stuff is because she's a dressmaker. People say she's a marvel with her needle. She's made lots of things for me

'PINKALOW'
AUGUST 20TH

dearest darlingest Pixie I am x←cross

becoz my 🏠 is full of 📦📦 and all

my best 👕←sparkly clothes are packed in the boxes

Everything is a BIG M U D←muddle
                                D E

Also Petal 🐾 got muddy and

stamped all over my 🛏️←bed

and now he's

on my pillow — NICE —

I don't think. U will ✒️←write loads

POST ←full of letters When we move, won't

you??? PROMISE???

♡ U 4 EVER Fizzy

xxxxx

and she made Jack the Splat a sailor suit once, but mostly she makes clothes for other people. Sometimes she makes great big fat, frilly party dresses.

I can sew too. Mum taught me when I was little, and it's good because now I can embroider on my clothes and make them look different from everyone else's. FRIDGEY COOL!

sailor suit

I've sewn sequins on my slippers and different

Socks with rubies

coloured buttons all over my jumper. My mum had some rubies left over from a dress she was making and she gave them to me. I sewed them on to my socks. GLAMOUROONY!

Jack (The Splat) Reenie Baz Fizzy

Petal

I love Pixie loads but I don't want to dress like her. I know friends who always want to be dressed the same, but Pixie and I are not like that. Oh, no! If Pixie's got blue jeans and a red jumper, then I ask my mum to make me a red skirt and a blue belt. We're 'individual', my mum says.

My mum's very cuddly. She's taught me loads of things besides sewing. Her biggest thing is telling me that I must never tell untruths. She says, 'Fizzy, you must never, ever tell fibs – that's one of the worst things you can do. If you tell Big Fat Fibs no one will ever know when you are being truthful . . .'

My mum's real name is Reenie, but Dad calls her 'Princess'. He often gives her a hug and says, 'Nothing's too good for my Princess,' which is really BLUSHIFYING. She calls my dad 'Elvis', not because it's his name – his name's Baz – but when he's

blushifying hug

11

doing his decorating he likes to pretend that his paintbrush is a microphone, and he makes all these drunken-monkey sort of moves. He sort of swings his bottom around and knocks his knees together, and sings old Elvis Presley songs. Then my mum says, 'OOOh, my Elvis, Elvis, Press Me!', and they have another great big hug. This can be really, REALLY EMBARRASSING – it sort of makes my toes curl.

THE KING

Baz making his 'moves'

3

Pop Went
the Weasel

'Viva Las Vegas!' says Dad.

Dad says 'Viva Las Vegas!' quite often. Usually he says it when he's dropped his paint pot, but this time he's said it because of this enormous crash, bang and wallop from our new next-door neighbour.

'There's old Ma Fossil throwing things around again!' he says. 'I expect she'll

BAZEEN
AUGUST 27TH

♡ ♡ ♡ ♡
dearest darlingest Pixie ♡ This is my new
— HUGE. It has a garden
With 🌸🌸🌸 and my
room has 2 🪟s. My dad is
🖌️ PAINTing everything different colours.
~~~COOL~~~

Mrs Fossil lives next door. She is a
bit 🦇 ←bat y but ☺nice☺. I have
made petal 👂 ←ear flaps. They have
EMERALDS on them. The Splat
has a cold 👃 nose YUCK!!!
love u 4 ever
xxxx FIZZY

need me to be on the mend before too long . . . "Well, blessa my soul . . . I'm all shook up . . ."' He sings this last bit. It's from one of his Elvis songs. He makes his knees do this wobbly thing, and then he and I and Petal go next door to see if Mrs Fossil is OK.

Petal with emerald-studded ear-flaps

I like Mrs Fossil's house. It's sort of dark and crumbly and full of STUFF. Our new house isn't very full of stuff because we only had a bungalow before and now we have big spaces between all the furniture. My dad's using up all his old paint to 'cosify' the place. He's done loads of spots and stripes and squiggly bits in all different colours. He's painting my room green with giant purple and pink flowers all over it. FANTASIBRILL!

'Are you lonesome tonight, Mrs Fossil?' croons my dad as Mrs Fossil's door creaks open. Don't know why he says that. It's only 10 a.m. Think it might be from another Elvis song.

'You, Mr Baz Pink,' says Mrs Fossil, 'are a caution! How did you know you're just the person I need? And young Frizzy here – come in, come in, do!' I've told Mrs Fossil loads of times that my name is 'Fizzy' and not 'Frizzy', but Dad says she's a bit 'mutton jeff', which means deaf.

Stuffed weasel

Either Mrs Fossil or the door creaks as it closes, and my dad and I stumble our way along her hall. She's got a whole collection of stuffed weasels in here. They are sort of balanced on branches that she's nailed to the wall. First time I saw them I thought they were dead creepy – well, they were definitely dead – but now I quite like them and they look good with the stuffed bear she's got in the corner.

Mrs Fossil's a bit crumbly too. Her hair's all grizzly and frizzly, and she pongs a bit in an old-lady sort of way.

'There I was,' says Mrs Fossil, 'just minding my own business, watching the racing on the telly, when – kerrrump – this china dog decides to throw itself across the room and smash in two! I don't know how it happened, I'm sure . . .'

My dad gives me a wink because, even

Stuffed bear

though we've only lived here such a short time, we both know how it happened. Mrs Fossil gets very excited watching the racing and she waves her arms around a lot 'like an 'orrible octopus', my dad says, and she knocks things all over the place without realizing.

Luckily, my dad has brought the glue with him, so he starts mending the china dog and Mrs Fossil gives me a chocolate biscuit.

'So, Frizzy – all excited about going to your new school then?'

I say, 'Orrrumph,' partly because my mouth is full of biscuit, but also because I don't want to think about going to my new school. It sounds HORROR-VOLTING. My mum says it's 'dead smart', but who wants to be dead smart? Not me. I think she means posh and I certainly don't want to be that either.

When I've finished my mouthful (my mum says it's disgusterous to talk with your mouth full), I say, ' Oh, yes! I can't wait to go. It sounds so exciting. They're going to put me in the top class, you know, on account of me being so incredibly clever and more talented than anyone they have ever had at the school before.'

Mrs Fossil says, 'Eh? What's that you say?' And I hear my dad clearing his throat very loudly. I think, Oops-a-bloomin'-daisy (as Dad would say), that was definitely a Big Fat Fib, so I quickly add, 'Actually, it sounds horrorvolting and I don't want to go at all. My mum's making my new uniform. It's really boring.'

'What, no nice frilly bits?' asks Mrs Fossil.

'Nope,' I say, 'and nothing sparkly.'

'What a shame,' she says, with a twinkle in her baggy old eye. 'You're good at sewing, aren't you, Frizzy?' I look at Mrs Fossil and she's smiling while she looks at my jeans. I've put diamonds and rubies all along the seams and embroidered a green snake on my pocket to remind me of Pixie. Then Mrs Fossil looks up at me, smiles some more, and I smile back. Think she's about to say something else, but Dad interrupts.

'There we are,' he says, 'right as nine pence,' and he hands Mrs Fossil her mended dog. Mrs Fossil gives me another chocolate biscuit and a little nudge when we say goodbye.

'Mind how you sew,' she says, and for some reason she seems to find that very funny. She cackles away. I think it would be polite to laugh too, so I do.

Dad and I sing 'Ain't Nothing But a Hound Dog . . .' down Mrs Fossil's hall. Dad does one of his 'moves' as we arrive back in our new kitchen, which he is in the middle of painting with yellow, orange and red stripes, and a few pink dots here and there 'just to jollify things a bit'. To accompany his 'move' through the kitchen door he sings the bit from a different song that goes 'Oh Let Me Be Your Teddy Bear . . .' and Mum squeals.

'OOOOh! If it isn't Elvis himself! Come on, Elvis, Press Me!' And they do one of those blushifying hug things.

'Elvis, I just love this

Mrs Fossil

house!' says Mum. 'It's too good to be true!'

'Nonsense,' says Dad. 'Nothing's too good for my Princess.' And he gives her a little pat on the bottom. Mum's bottom is quite big in a nice sort of way and it wobbles a bit when Dad pats it. Don't really want to see them being lovey-dovey-slushypups, so I think I'll go and paint a few extra pink blobs in my new bedroom. First I bend down to straighten Petal's earflaps, and Mum says, 'There's a letter for you – came while you were out. I popped it on your pillow.'

BRILLYBAGS! It must be from Pixie. I whizz upstairs and carefully open the pale blue envelope. Got to keep all Pixie's letters safe for our book.

Pixie says her pet snake ate three dead mice yesterday and that she misses me. She also says that her mum bought her some of those trainers with flashing lights. Feel a bit poo about this. I mean, I would have loved some flashing footwear, but I don't want to be a copycat. Think perhaps I'll sew some silver stars on to my new school trainers. That should make me feel better.

I decide to go and look in Mum's bit bag for some shiny stuff to make the stars out of, then I suddenly remember Mrs Fossil asking me if my new school uniform had any frilly bits on it, and I think WOW! I KNOW WHAT I'LL DO!

I'll sparkle up my school skirt! I'll frilly up my school shirt! I'll sew rubies on my school tie! There's loads I could do! I'll make it the most glamouroony uniform in the ENTIRE UNIVERSE!

4

Twinkle, Twinkle, I'm a Star

I go into Mum's sewing room to have a dig around and see what I can find.

Her sewing room isn't really a sewing room. It's a bedroom that we don't need. Mum has put her sewing machine on her purple sewing table and arranged all the stuff she uses to make clothes in piles on the shelves.

I love this room almost as much as my

dearest most darlingest Pixie

y Mrs Fossil broke her [china dog] So Dad [GLUE]d it 4 her. She gave me a jabberoony [idea]

My [eye] [deer] is to make my new school uniform :sparkly: I don't want to go to school without U but, I will feel better if my [coat] is :sparkly: is your pet [snake] [well?] [eye] think Petal stole one of Mrs Fossil's [weasels] She has loads- they are [weasel] stuffed!!

We had [eggs] 4 T - YUM!

l♥ve u loads 4 ever and ever
Fizzy xxxx

bedroom, except that Dad hasn't painted it yet. It's got all these really exciting things in it. There's this 'dummy' thing that looks like a body with no head and no arms or legs. It's what Mum uses to make clothes on. She puts what she's making on the dummy and then she sticks pins into it. It's very helpful, she says. At the moment it's wearing this huge pink and orange frothy dress.

Besides the dummy there are loads of shiny red boxes with big labels tied on with yellow spotty ribbons. All the labels have different things written on them. They say things like 'Gold Sequins'

frothy frock

and 'Large Rubies' and 'Frilly White Lace'. But my favourite box has a label that says 'Odds and Bods'.

'Odds and Bods' means leftover bits and pieces that Mum doesn't need any more. She lets me come and rummage in this box whenever I like.

Before I can really get going with my rummaging I have to go and see what's the matter with the Splat. I can hear him squawking in his room. He's supposed to be having a nap. But he isn't. I find he's thrown all his toys on to the floor and his nose is all snotty and disgusterous.

I lift him out and carry him to Mum's sewing room. I put him on the floor and give him some cotton reels to play with.

He looks quite happy – except for his nose. But I mean, even a fabberoony older sister like me has to draw the line somewhere, and wiping the Splat's scummy nose is where I draw it.

I find the shelf where Mum has put the boring old school uniform she made for me, and I pull out the blazer and have a look at it. DULL. DULL. DEADLY DULL.

I get the Odds and Bods box down and set to work.

A little while later I say, 'OK, Splat! What do you think of this?' I hold up the school blazer and I show him how fridgey cool I have made the badge on the pocket. The Splat doesn't say anything. He's chewing one of the cotton reels.

'It's so glamouroso, isn't it?' I carry on. 'Look, I've put a bit of pink frilly lace here and sewn some huge silver sequins on this boring bit here, and now I'm going to sew three sapphires along the top of the pocket. Super duper or what?'

The Splat isn't a great deal of help at times like these. He doesn't say much. Petal has just waddled in, so I show my new creation to him. He snuffles a bit before going to lie next to the Splat. I think that means he likes it.

I look at my blazer. I put it on and twirl around a bit in front of the mirror. It looks so glamouroony. It would be such a shame if my blazer pocket was the *only* little bit of my uniform that was sparklified . . . after all, it should all match, shouldn't it? I decide, there and then, that there is only one thing to be done . . . I go back to the shelf where Mum has stored the rest of my uniform. I find the skirt and pull it out.

It takes a jolly long time to do all the glittery gorgeous things I need to do to make my boring school uniform interesting. I have to sew masses of diamanté and rhinestones inside the pleats of my skirt to make it even halfway fabberoony. Then I stick loads of sequins on to the buttons on my shirt and finish up the decoration on my blazer with some little snippets of silver and gold lace and some trimmings on the sleeves. Then, very best of all, I find some silver glittery stars that I stick on to my trainers. They look like magic shoes when I've finished. This is going to be the most glamouroony school uniform in the whole wide world and the ENTIRE universe!

'Fizzy Freckles!' calls Mum up the stairs. 'I can't hear a single squeak – is Jack all right? What are you up to?'

I have to answer really fast because I don't want Mum to come up and see what I've done.

'He's fine,' I shout back. 'He's here with me. I managed to rescue him from a really ferocious dragon that had somehow got into his bedroom. It was terrible, but I was dead brave and shooed the dragon away. And now I'm playing peek-a-boo with the Splat . . .'

'Are you?' shouts Mum. 'Really, honestly?'

'Well, sort of,' I reply, because I think Mum has guessed that the peek-a-boo thing might be a bit of a Big Fat Fib, to say nothing of the dragon. How come she always seems to know when I make things up?

'So, what are you really doing?' she shouts up the stairs again.

Ooops-a-bloomin'-daisy! I've got to think fast. 'I *am* playing with the Splat,' I say, peering round the sewing-room door. 'I was just about to put him back in his cot – I'll be down in a mini-minute.' Then I whizz the Splat back into his own room and put him in his cot, dash back into Mum's sewing room and scoop up my sparklified uniform and my trainers, hurtle into my room and shove the whole lot under my bed, before I saunter, cool as anything, down the stairs.

5
Why Can You Never Find a Gnome When You Need One?

'Wakey, wakey, rise and shine,' says my mum as she pulls back my glittery pink bedroom curtains the next morning. 'Can't have you wasting this beeeeautiful morning in the land of nod. Up you get . . . we've got all those nametapes to sew on. Then we can go for a gorgeous little treat as it's the last day of the holiday.'

'Oooooh!' I say. My tummy does a somersault. The reason for this is:

a) Because I had forgotten that I have to go to school TOMORROW.

b) Because I had forgotten that Mum and Dad said they would take me and the Splat out for a special treat.

c) Because I don't know if I am excited or maybe the weeniest bit scared about Mum seeing how I've glitteryfied all my school stuff.

Obviously, I don't want Mum to see that I might be scared. I mean, it's not so much that I'm scared exactly. No. Because NOTHING scares Fizzy Pink . . . EVER . . . OK? It's more that I can't quite imagine what Mum will do next . . .

What Mum does next is leave the room

(phew!), and I get up and put on my most sparkly T-shirt and my fave jeans. Then I go down to the kitchen. When I get there Dad is painting more pink spots and singing 'Jailhouse Rock' to the Splat, who is splattering his soggy cereal. I'm trying to find somewhere to sit where the Splat can't reach me when Mum comes bustling in and says, 'The most extraordinary thing! I can't find your uniform anywhere, Fizzy. Have you gone and hidden it?'

'Oh, NO!' I say. 'I think something dreadful might have happened to it! Last night I heard weird noises and when I looked out of my bedroom door I saw all these gnomes going into your sewing room. Obviously, I shouted at them to stop, but they just went on. Then I crept up, incredibly bravely, and peeked round the door, and there they were – throwing things out of the window. I think they might have thrown my uniform out and then taken it off to their mountain hideout . . .'

My dad has stopped singing. The Splat has stopped splattering. Even Petal has stopped snoring.

'Erhem,' says Mum. 'WHAT was that you said, Fizzy?'

She's glaring at me now and so is Dad. The Splat is glaring too.

'Oh . . . I . . . um . . . said that . . . um . . . I think my uniform is under my bed where I put it last night . . .'

'And all that stuff and nonsense about gnomes was a fib, wasn't it?' says Mum. I nod my head.

'Really, Fizzy,' she says. 'I don't know what we're going to do with you!'

Honestly, it's not my fault! I don't know where they come from sometimes. I mean, I just open my mouth to say something dead ordinary and something else pops out. It's *really not* my fault. I think I might be possessed by an evil Big Fat Fib Fairy who won't let me out of her clutches . . .

'Well, go and fetch your uniform straight away and we won't hear any more of this stuff and nonsense about gnomes. All right?' My mum's using her strict voice and her neck's gone all pink. It does that when she's really cross. I go upstairs and fumble about under my bed.

My uniform still looks fabberoony this morning, but I'm not sure what Mum will make of it.

I go back to the kitchen.

'Here's my uniform,' I say, sort of quickly flashing it past her.

'Wait just a minute,' says Mum. 'Why is your school uniform sparkling?'

'Oh, did you see a sparkle?' I ask. 'That was probably one of those fairies that were fluttering in the garden earlier. You get loads of them round here. I expect it just flew in through the window by mistake –'

'Fizzy . . .' says my mum with this big frown, 'you know full well how I feel about fibs! Let me see the blazer.' She puts out her hand and I give her my blazer. I sort of hold my breath. She looks first at the blazer. She doesn't say a word. Then she makes me hand over the shirt with the sequins on the buttons, and finally the skirt with all the diamanté inside the pleats. I haven't brought my trainers down. I like them the very best. Think I might keep them a secret. I look at the ceiling. And wait.

'Well, I never!' she says.

I'm thinking, Well, I never what? Well, I never saw anything so glamouroony, or well, I never would have believed my daughter *could* be so naughty?

I wait. Again.

Mum goes on looking at the blazer. Dad doesn't move a muscle and the Splat sniffs.

I go on waiting.

I look hard at Mum and I think I can see a little SMILE . . . No, that can't be right, can it?

I wait a bit longer and finally Mum says, 'I don't know what your teachers

are going to make of you, I'm sure! You really are an individual and no mistake.'

And that's it! She hands me back the blazer without saying anything else.

Did I hear her say I was unbelievably naughty and that I must never do anything like this ever, ever again? I don't think so.

'Look,' says Mum finally, 'you've left a thread hanging here – run and fetch the scissors and we'll snip it off before we sew on the nametapes.'

PHEW!

Dad starts singing 'That's the Wonder, the Wonder of You . . .' and I beetle off to find the scissors.

When we've done all the nametapes, which doesn't take that long on account of both Mum and me sewing at the same time, Mum says it's time the Splat had a nap before we go out for our treat. She carries him upstairs and I look at all my newly marked stuff. My nametapes don't say 'Felicity Amber Jade Pink' because that would be too long and they don't say 'Fizzy Pink' because I wanted something a bit more mysterious. What they do say is 'F. A. J. Pink', which you've got to admit is pretty cool.

I decide to use the Splat's naptime to write to Pixie. I need to tell her about my school uniform and about the Petal's new toy. It's a stuffed weasel and I have a nasty feeling that it *might* have come from Mrs Fossil's front hall.

By the time I've finished writing to Pixie (which was quite hard to do as Mrs Fossil was making such a noise next door . . . maybe she's noticed that there's a weasel missing), and put all my pencils in the dark green velvet pencil case with the pink and yellow flowers I embroidered on it, the Splat is awake.

Can't wait to see what our treat is going to be. Maybe we're going to go swimming at the seaside . . . Or having a picnic in the country with big fat sandwiches and jelly babies . . . Or going

dearest darlingest Pixie

Bazeen
September 3rd

👁 did it !!!
👁 made my school 🦄 ←unicorn
sparkly — it's fabberoony. Also
I made a scarf 4 ♡♡ ←Petal's
weasel → 🐱. 2 morrow 👁
have 2 go 2 school — POO —
without U — double Poo. The
Splat splattered porridge in Dad's
☕ ←tea he was so X ←cross his
eyebrows got tangled 〰️〰️ ←tangle
                         ↑eyebrow
We are going on a treat soon — wish
U were coming. I ♡ U — write
soon pleeeeeeeease Fizzy
        xxxxx

to the pet shop to look at the guinea pigs . . . Or going to a cafe for lunch . . .

'Come on, Fizzy,' shouts Dad from downstairs. 'Time to shake a leg and brush up your feathers. We're off to the greatest place on earth – we're off to . . . The Rock 'n' Roll Museum!'

The WHAT?

6

Fossilized
Fruit Cake

Well! I won't bother going into all the
details about the Rock 'n' Roll Museum. It
was all about frosty old people from
years back who sang potty old songs like
the ones Dad sings. In fact the most
interesting part about it was that Dad
was crooning away as we went round
this museum and when we got to the bit
about Elvis Presley some batty old lady

suddenly shouted, 'Elvis Lives! He's here! He's alive and well and living in our town!' Then she came over all peculiar and started sort of fainting and going 'Oooooooh, Elvis!'

It was dead embarrassing. Dad and Mum didn't think so. I think Dad was quite pleased. Not because the lady was fainting, but because she thought he was Elvis. Mind you, he did have one of his Elvis outfits on. Mum has made him loads. They're all covered in jewels and shiny bits.

When she came round from the faints Dad sang the lady a little song called 'Love me Tender',

Baz in homemade Elvis outfit

and all these people crowded round to listen. I hid behind Mum and pretended I didn't know him, but he was actually fantasibrill. When he finished everyone cheered and clapped and said things like:

'You could be the King' (whatever that means).

And 'What a beautiful voice – you should be a Rock 'n' Roll star!'

Dad just smiled and said, 'No, no, Baz Pink's the name, painting's the game! Any colour as long as it's pink, that's what I always say.' And he started handing his business cards out to everyone.

Now that we're back from the Rock 'n' Roll Museum, Mrs Fossil has come to have tea with us. She's a bit upset because she's discovered that one of her weasels is missing. I give Petal a Look, but Petal doesn't seem to notice and I decide to keep quiet.

'I don't know when it happened,' says Mrs Fossil, 'but suddenly, there it was – GONE.' Mum tries to make her feel happier with a slice of her pink cherry cake.

'Thanks everso,' says Mrs Fossil, before going on to tell us all about her corns and how she is a slave to them. It's weird what grown-ups like to talk about. Mind you, she does go on to say some very interesting things about her first day at a new school, when she was my age, about 400 years ago.

corns

'There I was,' she says, 'quaking to the soles of my feet, but I thought to myself, "I'm not going to let anyone see how scared I am," and do you know what I did, young Frizzy? No? Well, I stood up in front of the whole class and said that they were lucky to have me there, and that I was a very extraordinary person and that I didn't mind who knew it. Well, I can tell you, it worked a treat! After that they treated me like I was royalty.'

Mrs Fossil's eyes go all crinkly as she cackles to herself and stuffs another piece of Mum's cake into her mouth. Her telling me that stuff about her first day at a new school has made me quite excited about tomorrow and I say, 'Would you like to see my new school uniform, Mrs Fossil?'

'What, the boring one with no frilly bits and no sparkle?' she asks.

'That's the one,' I say, and I dash upstairs to collect the skirt and shirt and blazer (I still don't think I'll show anyone the shoes).

'Well, I never did!' she says when I bring my new sparklified uniform down again.

'There's a sight for sore eyes if ever I saw one! You must be everso proud of little Frizzy here,' she says, looking at Mum and Dad.

Mum and Dad look at each other. There's a pause. I hold my breath.

'She's certainly an individual,' says Mum at last. 'I'll say that for her. She's an individual and no mistake.'

dearest darling Pixie

This is my second letter 2 u 2day. 👁

have 2 go 2 🍼 ←bed now and when I wake up I have to put on my 🦄 uniform and go to school WITHOUT U

Do U miss me ??? 💕←Petal

sat in some PAINT and now he has a pink ω ←bottom (ha, ha) How did your 〰 get into the washing machine?? He must B very clean now.

♡ve you loads and loads

PS The treat was 🩲 ←Pants

FiZZY xxxx

7

Dim Witties and Diamanté

The next morning I say goodbye to Mum and Dad, and climb out of Dad's pink van. As they drive away, Mum's nose is as pink as the paintwork and I think she's going to cry. Don't know why. I'm fine. I really am FINE. It's just – how am I supposed to know where to go? I mean, it would be *nice* if someone said, 'Hello! Shall I take you to your classroom?'

A girl with big blue eyes comes up. 'Hello!' she says. 'Shall I take you to your classroom?'

'Oh! OK,' I say, not wanting to sound too keen.

It seems to be a long way, wherever we are going, and Blue Eyes keeps looking at me as we wander along the corridors. 'What's that you've got on your skirt?' she says, making it sound like I've spilt porridge down my front.

'Diamanté,' I say, and sneak a look her way to see if she's properly impressed.

She's GIGGLING!

How rude.

Decide not to bother talking to her any more. I mean, anyone who doesn't recognize real diamanté when it's twinkling happily away in front of them must be way less than intelligent.

Blue Eyes leaves me outside a blue

door. It has a label on it that says:

5C
Class Teacher
Mrs SCary
^

I look at the label – eek! I jolly well hope that whoever added that 'S' was trying to be funny. Well, anyway, she's not going to frighten *me*, this Mrs SCary – oh, no! I'm about to go in when a curly-haired lady arrives. She has round pink cheeks and steel-rimmed glasses with steely little eyes behind them. Her eyes are like Pixie's pet snake's – cold as ice cubes. She opens her thin, bright-red mouth. 'AH!' she says, with her steel rims glinting off my sparkly bits. 'You must be Felicity. I'm Mrs Cary.'

I have to explain to her straight away

that even if someone shouted, 'Felicity, if you come here now you can have fifteen slices of chocolate cake and a bag of gobstoppers!' I would not move a single inch.

'My name is Fizzy, Fizzy Pink,' I say, putting out my hand. 'How d'you do?'

Mrs SCary makes a kind of hissing noise and ushers me into the classroom. 'Good morning, girls and boys. I'd like to introduce you all to our new girl, FELICITY.' She glares at me as she says this and I glare back. I mean, I've just told her, haven't I, about being called

Mrs SCary

Fizzy? So why can't she remember? Anyway, I haven't got time to put her right again as I have to look round the classroom and check everyone out.

I stare at them and they stare back at me. No one says anything. Not very friendly, I'm thinking. Then a dead posh voice from the back pipes up with, 'OOOh, look! What have we got here? An early Christmas decoration?'

Everyone laughs, including Mrs Scary, and I realize that clearly not one person in this entire room is bright enough to recognize True Style when it's right in front of their noses. Dim witties, the whole lot of them.

Mrs SCary hisses again and the dim witties pipe down.

'Now, FELICITY,' she says, with a slimy little smile, 'perhaps you would like to tell the class a bit about yourself?'

I'm about to say, 'No, thank you very much,' all polite, when I remember Mrs Fossil's story about her first day at school, and I realize that this could be my big chance to show this lot that I am not a person to be laughed at. I decide to give them a few fascinating facts about ME.

'My name is Fizzy . . . ' I say, and there is a sort of snort from the back of the room. 'Fizzy Pink . . .'

'Sounds like an advert,' someone sniggers. 'Fizzy Pink is a sparkling New Drink . . .'

'AND I am almost ten years old,' I continue, only louder this time. 'And I have all my clothes specially made for me.'

That shuts them up. I can see Miss Christmas Decoration at the back sit up and take notice.

'So we see,' hisses Mrs SCary quietly in

my ear. 'I shall have to speak to you another time about your school uniform. We do not allow sequins to be worn as part of school apparel.'

'But the sequins reflect my personality, you see,' I whisper back. 'So I have to wear them really.' By now, Mrs SCary is beginning to turn a bit green and I see her swallowing hard.

I look back at the rest of the class. Now that I've got their attention I feel all sorts of words bubbling up in my throat without being invited. 'We've just moved from our stately home to a smaller house nearby . . .' I say. They're all staring at me now with their mouths flapping. 'My dad,' I continue, clearing my throat, 'is a pop star and my mum's a princess.'

MrSCary

Suddenly thinking that I might have

gone Too Far, I add, 'But you won't have heard of my dad. He was HUGE years ago, but he only does special performances now.'

There's a silence while I smooth down my diamanté-studded skirt. I'm beginning to feel a bit sick when the very same Little Miss Christmas Decoration shouts out, 'Wasn't

sequins

that your mother in that, that pink VAN this morning? She didn't look much like a princess to me!' There's a

buttons

wheeze of giggling and some pig-like snorts.

'That was my driver.'

The words are out before I can do anything about them. For a moment I think that it might be all right because my mum DOES drive me sometimes after all. But then I begin to panic about all the other things I've said.

I try opening my mouth really wide to see if I can gulp the words back like a great big balloon of bubble gum. No such luck. That's it. Job done. Great Big Fat Fibs. The sort of whopping fibs that Mum has told me NEVER to tell. I swallow hard and try my Confident Smile but my lips get all stuck to my teeth.

'Well,' says Mrs Scary, 'thank you, FELICITY. That was extremely informative.'

I look up and see ice darts flashing from her eyes.

'I'm sure we will all look forward to meeting your famous parents and to hearing more about your stately home.'

More muffled giggling and then a girl with a red bow in her hair says, 'Do you have a pehnie? Nearly all of us here have pehnies.'

WHAT? What on earth is a 'pehnie' when it's up a flagpole (as Dad would say)? Is it another word for a brother? If so, I've got one of those. I'm just about to open my mouth and very likely to put my foot in it when Mrs SCary says, 'Now, now, children, this is not the time to discuss horsemanship.'

Horsemanship? Pehnies? Got it! They mean 'PONIES'. Well, I definitely haven't got one of those. I mean, what would be the point? You can't sew sequins on your clothes while you're sitting on a pony, can you?

I can't think what to say and I'm so grateful to Old Scary Snake for saving me from making another massive bloomer that when she says, 'FELICITY, you may go and sit down now,' I do exactly as I'm told.

8

Mrs SCary Has a Canary (i.e. She Gets REALLY Cross)

After registration we have maths, which is deadly dull! Spend my time looking round the classroom and writing to Pixie.

Miss Christmas Tree Decoration is actually called Camilla – dead posh, and her friends (don't know how she's got any of those) call her 'Cammy'. And they laughed at MY name! I mean, thank you very much, but Fizzy is a way less stupid name than Cammy.

'Felicity . . . FELICITY.' Mrs SCary seems to be looking at me, but she's obviously forgotten what my proper name is.

'Was there something you wanted, Mrs SCary?' I ask sweetly. 'Because if there is, perhaps I could remind you that my name is Fizzy. That's spelt F-I-Z-Z-Y.' I smile my most glamouroony smile. The rest of the class seems to be playing dead donkeys. At least, no one is speaking or moving or even breathing much (except one of the

Cammy

dearest darlingest Pixie

My new school is ◌ ←PANTS I have
a teacher called Mrs Cary. She looks
like your pet snake 🐍 but not as
friendly. ←hisssss The girls in my class are
all stuck up and they go around with their
noses in the air 👃←Nose and the boys
are PATHETIC. One of the girls is called
~~Clammy~~ Cammy and she said I looked
like a Christmas decoration 🔮
which proves that she doesn't know
-STYLE- when she sees it.
The Splat Sploshed yoghurt
in my trainers this morning—NICE I DON'T
THINK. Write to me soooooon. Miss you
loads. Loveyaloads. Your bestest
ever friend FIZZY

♡ x x x x x

boys, who's snoring.)

'Yes, FELICITY, there was something I wanted,' growls Mrs Scary. 'I wanted you to tell me the answer to the mathematical problem that I have written up on the board . . . . IF you would be so kind.'

I look at the board. It's got some gobbledegook on it. I take a deep breath.

'I'm most terribly sorry, Mrs SCary, but my brain doesn't do maths.' There's a gasp from the rest of the class and Mrs SCary looks as if she might explode. I'm just about to say that what my brain does best is sewing when the mid-morning bell goes and everyone starts getting out their snacks for break.

'FELICITY,' screeches Mrs SCary, 'come to the front of the class, please. I wish to speak to you. Now!'

By this time I notice that everyone has

scuttled out of the room, as if they know something terrible is going to happen. Everyone, that is, except a really miserable-looking girl, who has stringy plaits, a runny nose and a jersey with big holes in it. She stays cowering in the corner while I go up to Mrs SCary's desk.

'I WILL NOT HAVE INSUBOR-DINATION!' she hisses when I get up to her. I think about asking whether 'insub . . .', whatever she said, is some kind of medical thing, but as she is sort of shaking and looking a bit pale and wrinkly I decide it would be kinder not to mention illnesses.

'OK,' I say.

'NO, IT IS NOT OK!' she barks, and I really think that she might be about to burst into flames because now she's gone this really bright red colour, a bit like the stripes Dad is painting in the kitchen.

'You will take a detention,' she wheezes.

Crumpets! What's a 'detention' when it's at home? Does she mean that she's going to put me in prison? No one ever got put in prison at my last school and I was there for ages – I've only been here for half a day so far.

I must be looking puzzled as she sighs wearily and says, 'That means, after you have eaten your lunch you will stay in and write out fifty times "I must not be rude to my teacher". Do you understand, FELICITY?'

NO. I do not understand. When was I rude? Mind you, I don't really want to go trotting round the playground being 'pehnies' with all the dim-witty girls in my class, and none of the boys are worth bothering about. Might as well stay in and do some writing. If I write fast I might be able to write to Pixie as well . . .

'Yes, Mrs SCary,' I mumble, and Mrs SCary sighs loudly, gets up and leaves the room.

'I could sit with you when you do your lines, if you like,' says a little voice behind me. 'I don't mind . . .'

I realize that the voice is coming from the holey-jumper girl in the corner. She looks sort of pleadingly at me and I think, well, I suppose it might be nice to have SOMEONE to talk to, even if it is only Stringy Plaits.

Nobody else talks to me much before lunch break. I see Cammy whispering to one of the other stuck-up dim witties and pointing at me during history (which, thanks to Mrs SCary, is also deadly dull). I pretend not to notice. When the bell goes for lunch one of the boys comes up

and asks if my dad has won any gold
discs for his singing.

'Oh, loads,' I say. 'We've got
so many gold discs we could
have covered the walls of our
stately home with them.'

'Wow!' he says, and he looks
quite impressed. In fact he's
not the only one who suddenly
seems to think that I'm worth
talking to. By now Cammy
and a couple of the other
girls have come up to me
too, and they make a sort of
circle round me. But I'm not
scared. Honestly, I'm not . . .

'So,' says Cammy, 'does
your mother wear her crown
all the time?' The other two
girls are sniggering behind
their hands.

Stringy
Plaits

'Of course,' I say.

'What, even when she does the hise work?' Cammy asks, and the other two girls are snorting into the sleeves of their jumpers. I haven't a clue what she's talking about, but obviously I can't let on. What is 'hise work' when it's at home? Is it something to do with 'pehnies', I wonder . . . perhaps 'hise' means 'horse'.

I'm about to tell them that, unlike many royal people, my mum doesn't ride when Stringy Plaits, who is standing behind me, says, 'Fizzy's mother has lots of servants to clean their house.'

'Doesn't she?' she asks, turning to me. I just stare at her. She gives me a little shy sort of smile. Honestly, if it wasn't for the fact that Stringy Plaits obviously has no fashion sense I could have hugged her. Cammy meant 'HOUSE work', but she had somehow squidged the word.

'Naturally,' I say. 'We have many servants. My mother doesn't need to lift a finger. In fact, she finds it quite tiring enough telling all the people who work for her what to do. She wouldn't dream of doing any 'hise' work herself.' I stand up very tall with Stringy Plaits standing next to me, and I look Cammy straight in the eye.

'Oh, my, get you!' she says, but I think I must have been quite convincing because she and the other girls don't seem to be able to think of anything else to say to me. She turns to her friends and says, 'Let's leave FELICITY and Daisy and go and have lunch, come on.'

I look round, wondering who 'Daisy' is. There's only Stringy Plaits and me and a few boys left. Stringy Plaits must be Daisy . . . that's actually not a bad name. I look at her more closely and she looks at me and smiles a great big smile that makes two dimples appear, one on each side of her mouth. It's just possible, I suppose, that Daisy might not be *quite* as dim witty as the rest of them.

9

Snotty Snot and Batty Bats

Lunch is disgusterous, and I have to sit next to a teacher and be dead polite all the way through. I try my best. I manage not to tell any more fibs. Think I've probably told enough of those already today.

Back in the classroom, after lunch, I'm trying to remember what it was Mrs SCary wanted me to write fifty times.

'I think it was "I must not be rude to my

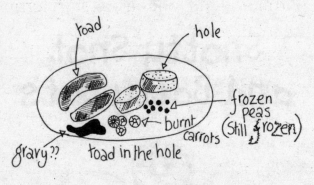

drawing of disgusterous lunch
to send Pixie

toad

hole

frozen
peas
(still frozen)

burnt
carrots

gravy??

toad in the hole

something
evil hiding
under custard

teacher",' says Daisy, who's followed me
in and must have noticed me frowning a
lot.

'Thanks,' I say, getting out some paper.

'I love your clothes,' says Daisy,
looking admiringly at the sparkly bits on
my skirt. Humph. Well, she may be the
only person in the entire school to
appreciate how fabberoony my uniform

is, but I still wish she would blow her nose. She's as bad as the Splat in the snot department and she is sitting terribly close to me.

'I really do think I'd better write these lines,' I say, 'or Mrs SCary will be even more angry with me . . . perhaps you could move over a bit?'

'Shall I write them for you? I will if you like,' says Daisy, and she finally blows her nose and pulls my bit of paper towards her. She starts scribbling away.

Don't know what to do now. I can't write to Pixie because all my letters to Pixie are Strictly Private and I don't want Daisy to see what I'm doing. I think about all the snobby girls and pathetic boys in my class and wonder if any of them are worth talking to.

Daisy straightens her holey jumper and finishes writing my lines for me. I realize that I will probably have to be nice to her now for ever and ever. POO.

For the rest of the afternoon I keep an eye on everyone to see if anyone else besides Daisy might be less dim witty than the others. It's not even worth considering the boys (because they're boys), so I concentrate on the girls. It looks like Cammy is a real bossyboots and all the other girls just do what she tells them. This means that if Cammy tells the others to be poopypants to me they will be.

Cammy hates me. I can see it in her eyes. She really, especially hates me in the sports lesson when I put on my gorgeous, most favourite trainers with the silver stars. All the other girls get dead excited about my trainers, but she says, 'I think silver stars are so babyish. I wouldn't be seen DEAD with stars on

MY shoes.'

After that, all the other girls stop being excited about my trainers and start saying things like, 'Oh, yes! That's just what I was thinking, Cammy – you're so right. Stars are just SO not cool!'

Well, I don't care. Why would I care? They are all so drippy that they have to agree with everything Cammy says. All except Daisy, that is, who says she thinks my shoes *are* cool. The rest of them can all go and jolly well get squashed by their 'pehnies' for all the difference it will

make to me. I wouldn't want to be friends with any of them anyway. SO THERE.

I manage to stop Mum driving right up to the front of the school when she comes to collect me. Don't want Cammy to see me getting into Dad's pink van again. Also, Mum's wearing her red-and-white spotty 'Capri' pants with a shocking-pink frilly T-shirt that she's made, which is not at all the sort of thing a princess would wear.

Mum says, 'So, was it wonderful? Did you have a gorgeous time?'

And I say 'It was fabberoony – I've made loads of friends already . . .'

'Really?' says Mum, and

she tries to give me a good hard look, but she can't because she's driving.

'Oh, yes,' I say. 'Honestly. They all really liked my uniform too, especially my trainers.'

'Oh, good, Fizzy Freckles. I'm so pleased,' she says, and she seems quite happy and sort of relieved, but I feel like a mouldy worm because I know I've told another Great Big Fib.

Dad says, 'So, was it all lovely jubbly at your new school then?' when I get home, and I have to tell him the same as I told Mum – that it was 'fabberoony' and that I 'loved every minute of it' – and he starts singing 'Jailhouse Rock', and luckily that seems to be that.

The Splat sploshes jam on to my history prep book, so I give it to Petal to lick off, and decide that I will go and pay

Mrs Fossil a visit instead of doing my homework. I mean, HOMEWORK? BORING.

'Well, it's my friend Frizzy,' she says as she opens the door. 'Come in, come in!'

I notice that Mrs Fossil has rearranged her weasels so that the gap where the missing one was doesn't show so much. I thought about trying to put the weasel back without Mrs Fossil noticing, but whatever Petal has done to it has made it look very peculiar. I feel really bad, but I don't want to get Petal into trouble.

'That looks nice,' I say

'Eh? What's that?'

'Your weasels look nice,' I repeat.

'Haven't got sneezles,' she says. 'I'm as fit as a flea. How was school?'

There's something about the way Mrs Fossil is looking at me, with her baggy old eyes all twinkling and wrinkling. I sit and stare at her for a bit and she stares back, and then I know that I will have to tell her the truth.

'It was horrorvolting,' I say. 'Nobody likes me except a girl with stringy plaits and a holey jumper, and my teacher looks like a snake and she got so cross that she nearly exploded, and some posh girl called Cammy said she had a 'pehnie' and that I looked like a Christmas decoration and that the stars on my trainers were babyish and the Splat has put jam on my homework and . . .'

'Just jealous,' says Mrs Fossil.

'What?' I say.

'Jealous. That Tammy girl.'

'What do you mean?' I ask, wondering if Mrs Fossil actually heard any of the things I've been saying.

'They're all jealous of you, that's all –

except that one with the thingy bats . . .

'Stringy plaits,' I say.

'Yes, that's the one. The rest of them are jealous of you, that's all. Want to be just like you, I wouldn't wonder . . . you mark my words, young Frizzy.'

I stop listening. I mean, obviously Mrs Fossil is completely and totally batty.

10

Sing-Along-A-Superstar

Things start 'smelling of roses' (as Dad would say) over the next few days (well, they begin to get slightly less pooey anyway). School is still the pits and Cammy still hates me, but the really whizzy thing is that Mrs SCary isn't there! The head teacher says she's had a turn and has to have several weeks off to get over it. I think she might have exploded, in which

dearest darlingest Pixie

Clammy is still being a ←PIG
and a stinky ←nose clothes peg girl wants
to be my friend.
gave me a detention ←Mrs Cary
and I ⟩HATE SCHOOL⟨ but I told
mum and dad that I ♥ ←love it.
Pleeeease send me a ←Photo
of U. I will send U one of me
and a ⋮SPARKLY⋮ ❀ ←flower
that I am making 4 U.
←fish U were here.
←Petal still has paint on
his botty!!!!
Love U 4 ever Fizzy xxxx

case she may NEVER come back. Instead of Mrs SCary we have a supply teacher called Ms Vine. When she introduces herself to us she tells us her name is Diana, which I work out pretty quickly makes her Ms D. Vine as in 'Divine', and she IS!

The most divine things about her are that:

a) She calls me Fizzy.

b) She says that she thinks my uniform is 'stunning'.

c) She doesn't only teach stinky maths and history, but she also teaches art, which is a proper subject, and singing, which almost is.

Miss Vine

*

I have to stand next to Daisy in our singing lesson. Well, I don't have to, but Cammy and her gang don't look at all friendly today and I don't really want to stand on my own. Obviously, what puts the others off is that I am way more sparkly and interesting than any of them and they don't want me to outshine them. Cammy tells everyone in our class, including Ms D. Vine, that my dad is a pop star.

'So, reeely, Ms Vine, you should make Fizzy sing the solo. She's sure to have a wonderful singing voice!' She then says 'Not', quiet enough so that Ms Vine doesn't hear it, but everyone else does and they all laugh. Except for Daisy, which is nice of her. So what? I don't care about any of them. Let them all laugh. They don't know yet that singing is one of my best things and I would be quite happy to sing a solo. So boo snubs!

'Very well then,' says Ms Vine cheerfully. 'Fizzy, why don't you start us off with the first verse of "The Sun Will Be Up Tomorrow" from the musical *Annie*? Open your mouth nice and wide and let's have a really big voice! Ready?' And she plinkety-plonks away on the piano for a bit before nodding to me to tell me it's time for me to begin.

Now, I don't want to be a big head, but I can sing. And I can sing loud. I mean, I can sing REALLY loud. So I do. While I'm singing, I sort of notice that the windows in the music room are rattling a bit and that even Daisy moves a little away from me.

When I finish there's a startled silence in the classroom, but then Ms Vine and everyone else start clapping and cheering. Everyone, that is, except Cammy. I look round at them all and give Cammy my biggest cheesy grin, and she looks poisoned daggers at me. Then I see her nudging the people around her and telling them to 'shut up clapping' and they do. They all stop one after the other and look dead embarrassed, and I hear some of the soppy girls saying 'Sorry' to Cammy.

I mean, WHY? Just because she's a big fat bossyboots doesn't mean they all have to do everything she tells them, does it?

'Don't listen to them,' whispers Daisy. 'I

thought you were fab.'

'Well done, Fizzy,' says Ms Vine. 'Now let's all sing the second verse together . . .' So we start, but while I'm singing away and thinking that Daisy really isn't that bad, I feel this jab in my back and I turn round and see clammy Cammy standing right behind me. She glares at me and mouths the words, 'Shut up NOW, or else!'

I wouldn't normally do anything a big pig like her would tell me, but this time she is standing right behind me and I can feel her hot breath on the back of my neck. I think it wouldn't be that hard for her to push me over in front of everyone and . . . and . . . Obviously, I'm not a bit scared, because I, Fizzy Pink, am never, EVER scared. But, anyway, I shut up. I stand there all through the rest of the singing lesson not singing. This is

BORING and ANNOYING. But, even worse than that, Ms Vine doesn't seem to notice.

11
Arty Party

Every day when I go home I tell Mum and Dad that everything is brillybags. I know this is a Big Fat Fib. Everything is grotty-bags, but I don't want them to know that. Daisy is the only thing that isn't completely grottybags. I was going to write and tell Pixie about her, but then I decided not to. Don't know why.

Last lesson on Wednesday we have art. GOOD. Art is my favourite lesson.

'Now listen, everyone,' Ms Vine says

♡ darlingest Pixie ♡

For my birthday I would like some ~worms~ ←worms to put down Clammy's neck and a stink (BOMB) to put in ← Mrs Cary's desk incase she comes back OR I would like a big [gift] ← Parcel with YOU inside !!!! Dad has painted the hall like a [rainbow] ←rain bow it's frikky cool but the Splat ○sploshed○ custard on some of it. ❀←Petal has buried his scarf [weasel] ← weasel. (Mrs Fossil's) ∴ Love U 4 ever and ever

Fizzy xxxxxx

when we are all sitting down. 'Today we are going to be doing "collage" portraits.'

Cammy's such a dim witty, she thinks 'collage' is a place where people go when they finish school. I mean, anyone with any brains at all knows that it means sticking different things down on a sheet of paper to make a picture. I try giving Cammy one of my confident smiles, but I'm not feeling very confident and it goes a bit wrong. She glares back at me.

'So,' says Ms Vine, 'I would like you all to collect as many different pieces of coloured paper and scraps of material that you want, and set to work making a portrait of someone. It can be anyone you like. It could be of you or your friend or brother or sister or even your pet . . . Now, off you go!'

FABBEROONY! Except that Cammy

barges in and grabs all the best sparkly stuff and most of the bright colours. By the time I'm able to reach anything, all that's left are boring old grey and brown bits and a tiny bit of silver foil.

I take my bits back to my table and set to work. While we're cutting and sticking and tearing, Ms Vine comes round to see what we're doing. She gets to Cammy's table and says, 'Some of you don't quite seem to have got the idea. I want to see a proper picture. Try to make your collage look like someone.' And she carries on walking round.

'Now, here,' she says, stopping at my table, 'this is what I'm looking for!' And she holds up my picture. 'You see, Fizzy, here is doing a wonderful picture of a warthog. Excellent, Fizzy, carry on.'

Well! I don't like to say, 'Actually, it's not a warthog. It's a portrait of Cammy,'

Cammy's Portrait

because Cammy looks cross enough as it is. So I just carry on and finish it off with a little sliver of silver in each of the eyes to give them an evil glint.

When I show my collage to Mum and Dad that evening and explain that it's of one of the girls in my class, Mum says, 'Bless my soul . . . poor little thing! Must be dreadful for her looking like that!'

(Dad is singing 'You're the Devil in Disguise', which seems like a good choice to me.)

'Oh, Fizzy, I feel everso sorry for this poor little love. What did you say her name was?' Mum asks.

'Cammy,' I say, and her name sort of sticks in my throat.

'Well, I tell you what. As it's your birthday on Saturday I think it would be gorgeous if you asked all the girls in your class to come here for a birthday sleepover. It would be SO jolly! You've made lots of new little girl friends and I think it would be wonderful to have all the darlings to stay – we could have lots of games and tea and cakes and jellies and balloons and ANYTHING you like . . . yes! You must invite them ALL, don't leave anyone out . . .'

'But, Mum,' I squeak, 'I don't –'

'Nonsense,' says my mum. 'It won't be any trouble – it'll be FUN and it'll give your dad and me a chance to meet all your new chums, especially poor little Cammy.'

'But . . .!' I squeak again.

'No, you're not to worry, Fizzy Freckles, your dad and I will have a smashing time getting everything ready. Now, why don't you go and make the invitations, then we can take them into school in the morning.'

OH, BUMPITS CRUMPETS!

12
The Trouble with Telling Big Fat Fibs by F. A. J. Pink (i.e. ME, Fizzy)

1. When you tell a tiny fib it often grows bigger and bigger without you doing anything to it.
2. When a fib has grown enormous (i.e. a BIG FAT FIB) it can be very difficult to make it go away. For

example, if you tell your mum and dad that you love your new school and you have loads of friends it's hard to say 'Oops-a-bloomin'-daisy!, I made a mistake – I hate my school and I haven't any friends.'

3. When you tell two Big Fat Fibs you can get squashed in between them. For example, like me, because now Mum and Dad want to ask all my school 'friends' (not) here for my birthday, and when my school 'friends' (not) come they are expecting Dad to be a POP STAR and Mum to be a PRINCESS!

4. If someone gets squashed between two Big Fat Fibs it is very difficult to know WHAT TO DO NEXT, for example, LIKE ME.

The End

P.S. I would rather be put in a

sandwich with a hard-boiled egg and be eaten than invite Cammy and her gang to my party.

13
Poop on My Party – Please

The next morning I feel like there's a great big fat hippo-bottymus sitting on my head and I haven't a clue what to do about my sleepover, i.e. The Party That is Going to Ruin My Life For Ever and Ever.

What I think I will probably do is sort of 'forget' to give out the invitations and then tell Mum and Dad that everyone is busy that afternoon and can't come.

I'll just have to cross 'all my little pinkies' (as Dad would say) and HOPE that Mum doesn't decide to change the date so that all 'my little friends' (not) CAN come.

'Goodness gracious, deary eyes, whatever's the matter with you this morning?' asks Mum as I plod into the kitchen. 'Didn't you sleep well? All excited about your party, I expect, was that it?'

'Orrrumph,' I say, because that's a good sort of word to use when you can't think of anything at all to say. And also the Splat has just splodged a big blob of strawberry yoghurt on to my foot.

102

'Well, don't you worry, Fizzy Freckles,' says Mum, mopping up the yoghurt. 'I can promise you it's going to be the best sleepover EVER. None of your friends will ever forget Fizzy's party, I can promise you that!'

'Great!' I say (but not meaning it), and I'm thinking that no one will ever remember my party because I'm not actually going to invite anyone. Obviously, I don't say this. Mum is looking through the invitations to make sure that I have spelt everything right. I mean, honestly, as if I wood spel anyfink rong, but that's a mum for you . . .

We're just driving into the school gates in Dad's pink van, with the Splat strapped in the back and Petal lying on my school bag on the floor, when I see Ms D. Vine. Mostly, I'm hoping that no one will ever

come to my birthday
Sleeᶻᶻᶻᶻᶻᶻover
on
FRIDAY
from
Fizzy PINK

see me arrive in our van, but I really like Ms D. Vine and when I see her I squeak, 'Oh, look! There's my new teacher.' And Mum bangs her foot on the brake and screeches to a stop right next to her.

I'm so surprised that I forget to hide under the seat. I see Mum jump out of the van with my invitations in her hand!

'Excuse me,' she says to Ms Vine. 'I'm

Fizzy's mum, and I wondered if I could ask you to give Fizzy's party invitations to all the little girls in her class – I thought perhaps at registration? I don't think Fizzy had much sleep last night and what with the overexcitement and all, I'm worried that she might forget . . .'

It's like watching a film in slow motion. I see Mum handing all my invitations to Ms Vine and I just sit there with my mouth flapping 'like a gate in a gale' (as Dad would say) when Ms Vine says, 'Of course, Mrs Pink, that will be a pleasure!' She doesn't say, 'I thought you were a princess,' or anything like that, which makes me like her even more.

But Ms Vine having my invitations is not AT ALL FUNNY.

I jump out of the car and say to Mum,'Don't worry about driving me any further. I'll walk from here.'

'Righty-ho!' she says. 'You walk in with Ms Vine then, and I'll see you later.'

This is GOOD. This means:

a) That no one will see me arrive in our pink van.
b) That I might be close enough to Ms Vine to somehow get the invitations back.

Not sure how to do this. Ms Vine is holding them tightly in her hand. I try bumping into her to see if she will drop them, but all that happens is that she says, 'Oh, dear! Are you all right, Fizzy? You must be very sleepy to be falling over your feet so early in the morning. You nearly made me drop your precious invitations and that would never do, would it?'

'No,' I say as I follow her into our classroom, feeling sick as a pig. I see her put my invitations on her desk and then she begins to clean the board and tidy things up. Perhaps I could sneak up now and sort of pinch them? Maybe I could grab them and throw them out of the window into the hedge outside?

Or I could stuff them up my jumper and pretend that they had just disappeared. Maybe I could EAT them. I've read about people 'swallowing the evidence'. Mind you, there are ten of them and they are quite big . . . I'm just creeping up to grab them still not knowing *quite* what I'm going to do when Ms Vine turns round. She sees me with my fingers all twitching above my invitations and she LAUGHS! She laughs a great big laugh and for a moment I think, 'PHEW! That's all right, she's going to let me swallow them.' But then she says, 'Don't worry, Fizzy, I was just going to get everyone sitting down and then we will give out your invitations. I know how excited you are about it! Come and stand by me . . .' I shuffle gloomily to Ms Vine's side.

'Now, children,' she says in her loud teacher's voice. 'I would like everyone to sit down quietly, while Fizzy here gives all you lucky girls one of her lovely party invitations.'

'OOOOO!' says Cammy in her snotty-nosed stuck-up voice. 'How jolly super, now we will get to see Fizzy's new hise and meet the princess and the pop star! Goody, goody!' And everyone laughs.

'Shh now, children,' says Ms Vine. 'I know you girls are all very excited about the prospect of Fizzy's party, but now is not the time to be discussing it. Carry on, Fizzy.'

And I have to do it! There, in front of everyone! I have to give Clammy Cammy an invitation to MY SLEEPOVER! My hand goes all wobbly as I give it to her, and she looks up at me with a snotty slobbog sort of smile and whispers, 'I wouldn't miss this for the world!'

OH, BOTHER.

14

Pixie's Petrifying Plan

All day my brain feels fuzzy. Daisy is the second one to say that she would 'love to come' to my sleepover and I feel glad that at least one person who is halfway decent is coming. But then the rest of Cammy's gang all say that they 'would simply ADORE' to come to my party too . . .

Oh, GULP! What am I going to do

now? One of the dim-witty girls even asks if we will be riding my 'pehnie' and I have to explain that I don't actually have a 'pehnie', but I am tempted to suggest that she could try and ride on Petal if she liked. At least that would be good for a giggle! (Not for Petal, though.)

By the time I get home I think I might have a terrible illness. Actually, this might not be a bad idea. If I had something deadly catching no one would want to come on Friday . . . I'm about to borrow some of Dad's paint and splodge big red paint spots all over my face when Mum says, 'Well, I expect all your little friends will bring you wonderful presents – not that you should be thinking about that, of course, but even so . . .'

GROTTYBAGS! That was something I hadn't really thought about! Presents! Might be a bit of a pity to be too ill to get any presents . . . Ooohhh, I wish I knew what to do.

I talk to Petal for hours, but he hasn't got any ideas. Then I suddenly think that one person who could possibly help is Pixie.

'Mum,' I say, trying my best to look as sweetie tweetie as pie. 'Do you think, as it's almost my birthday and I have been such a really, really good girl and kept my room tidy, sort of, and done all my homework, kind of, and as I did wash up last Monday, whether I could POSSIBLY, only for a short time, just MAYBE, phone Pixie?'

'I don't see why not,' says Mum. 'Just this once as it's your birthday.'

I rush to the phone and dial Pixie's number.

I know Pixie is my very best friend in all

the world but honestly, I mean, all she says is that I am a complete noodle brain to have told such gigantic fibs about my mum and dad. Then she says how could I possibly even think of having a party without her? And what's the point of having a party if you haven't got any friends to come? This is NOT HELPFUL. I think about telling Pixie that actually there is one person who I don't really mind coming to my party (i.e. Daisy), but instead I tell her that the party is more Mum and Dad's idea than mine. She says she doesn't care and that if I had even half a brain I would see that I have to tell the truth at some point, or everything is going to get worse and worse. ALL RIGHT. OK. THANK YOU VERY MUCH, BRILLIANT PLAN. I don't think.

Well, I can't, can I? I mean, tell the truth . . . Except, if I don't, Pixie might be right and it will all get worse and worse . . .

I sit on the floor of Mum's sewing room and look through the Odds and Bods box. Sometimes this can help me have an idea. Usually my idea would be to do with making something sparkly. Today I'm hoping I will have an idea about What To Do Next . . .

I've been in here for ages now and the only thing that keeps popping into my head is what Pixie said. She said, 'Tell your mum and dad what you have done or everything will get worse and worse.'

OK. This is it. I'm going downstairs and I am going to tell Mum and Dad the

Truth. My knees are all wobbly. But I'm going to do it. Because I, Fizzy Pink, am as brave as a lion and will never be afraid to stand up for myself. I think about Mrs Fossil and Daisy and that somehow makes me feel even braver.

'Why are you standing there with your mouth open, young Fizzy? Are you trying to catch flies?' asks my dad.

I've been standing in the kitchen, sort of gazing at the paintwork, for quite a long time.

'Or is it my paintwork that's got you all shook up?'

'Nnnnooooo,' I say.

'Well, what then?' asks Mum. They are both staring at me now.

This is it. Here I go. Gulp. I take a big breath and say, 'Itoldeveryoneatschool – thatmymumisaprincessandmydadisapop star.'

Done it! I wait for the explosion. Silence. Then Dad says, 'Hmmm, me a pop star, eh? I like the sound of that . . .' Mum gives him one of her Looks, and he stops smiling and tries to look dead serious.

'Felicity Amber Jade Pink.' (Mum only EVER calls me 'Felicity' when she is really horrorvoltingly angry with me.) 'I have never heard such a thing in all my life! You KNOW how I feel about fibbing and this is a gigantic Big Fat Fib if ever I heard one!' She has gone very pink and her chin's wobbling a bit. Even Dad is looking quite scary now – his eyebrows are all knotted together like a big hairy caterpillar.

'I don't know what to say, I'm sure,' Mum carries on. 'But there's one thing that's definite. As tomorrow is Friday, the very first thing you will do when you get to school is to tell all those nice little girls that you have told an ENORMOUS fib and that you are very, very sorry indeed.'

She stops for a bit and straightens her skirt. She and Dad look so grumpy that I think it might be a mistake to tell them that I have told even MORE fibs and that the girls at school aren't nice or little. They are nearly all huge and horrorvolting. Well, definitely horrorvolting anyway. Still, Mum and Dad will find that out soon enough. Then I wonder if anyone will want to come to my sleepover after I tell them the truth, but I realize that most of all I feel upset that Daisy will know that I'm a Great Big Fat Fibber.

15

Truth or Dare (or Both if You Happen To Be Me)

I had a scarifying nightmare last night! I dreamt that all the girls in my class looked like Cammy and they all came to my party. There were loads and loads of them and they were all laughing at me. And none of them bought me any birthday presents at all!

Had to check under my bed when I woke up to make sure there weren't any Cammys hiding there. Luckily, there was only Petal, but I still felt spooky when I got down to breakfast in the kitchen, even though TODAY IS MY BIRTHDAY!

'Well,' said Mum, after she had glared at me a bit, 'I know it's your birthday, but before we can let you have any presents at all we must be sure that you do the right thing when you get to school. And what is it that you have to do, Fizzy?'

'I have to tell everyone in my class the truth,' I say in my tiniest voice.

'That's right,' says Mum. 'Now, you *promise* me, don't you, that you will explain everything? If I find out that you haven't told all those nice little girls in your class that you told them all those Big Fat Fibs . . . I . . . I . . . I WON'T MAKE YOU A BIRTHDAY CAKE! So, what do

you think of that?'

What I think is that if I wasn't the bravest person in the whole wide world I might cry . . . But as it is, I just say, 'I promise I will tell everyone the truth.'

'Good girl,' says Mum. 'And here's a

birthday kiss for my birthday girl.' Then she gives me a great big smacking kiss, which she says is all the presents I'm going to get until my party this evening. EXCITING – I don't think.

Mum tries to jollify me as she whisks up my school bag and bundles me into the van. But I feel totally grottybags.

Everyone comes up to me when I walk into the classroom and wishes me happy birthday. I can see that all the girls have brought bags with their party clothes inside (and probably presents too), and it makes me feel dead wobbly.

I have to tell Ms Vine that I have something to say to the whole class and she makes me stand by her desk in front of all those snotty faces. It takes ages for her to shut them all up because Cammy keeps shouting things like, 'OOOOOh!

Look at the princess's daughter! Did she give you a palace for your birthday? Did you come to school in a golden coach or in that pink VAN?' Ha ha, very funny.

By the time she has finished my knees are all shaky, and even seeing Daisy smile and wave at me doesn't make me feel any better.

Then I have to do it. So I do. 'Actually, my mum's not a princess and my dad's not a pop star. I'm really sorry. I told everyone a fib . . .'

It's very quiet, and then Cammy says, 'Don't you think we all knew that anyway? You're SO sad!' And she laughs really loudly. She sounds like a piglet with tummy ache. No one else laughs. They all stare at me. But then Daisy says, so everyone can hear, 'Can we still come to your sleepover?'

'Oh, yes!' shout all the other girls. 'We

122

still want to come too!'

I can't believe it! I didn't think any of them would want to speak to me ever again, let alone still want to come to my party.

Daisy gives me a big dimply smile and I smile back. PHEW! Then I look at Cammy. She looks dead grumpy on account of the other girls still wanting to come to my sleepover. Then she says, 'Of course we all still want to come. It will be such fun to meet your reeeely ordinary parents who aren't A PRINCESS and A POP STAR!' And she does her piglet laugh again.

But I don't care because I've done it! I've told everyone the truth, and Ms Vine says, 'It's a very, very bad idea to tell people things that are not true. However, having said that, you've just done a very brave thing, Fizzy. Well done! You must always remember that little poem:

Oh what a tangled web we weave,
When first we practise to deceive.

But now that you *have* told the truth, I hope you have a very happy birthday.' And she hands me a birthday card with a picture of a puppy on it.

I think all the excitement must have gone to Ms Vine's head as I have no idea what she's talking about, but the card makes me feel a tiny bit better.

I still feel big pants about the party, though, now that Cammy is still going to come. I bet she makes the whole thing a gigantic disaster. She'll laugh at the way Dad's painted our house and she'll think my parents are 'reeely sad'. She'll probably be even nastier to me after my party and go on and on saying that my sparklified uniform makes me look like a Christmas decoration. And everyone will agree with her.

For the first time ever, I am NOT looking forward to going-home time.

16
Party Panic

At home time Dad has organized for us all to be picked up in a posh people carrier. The girls have their bags and we're going to change when we get to my house.

My tummy's all jelly at the thought of arriving at Bazeen and having Cammy be all snotty about it. The others are excited and making lots of noise, except for Daisy who is very quiet on the way to my home. I expect she's really upset about my big fat fibbing. I begin to feel sick.

Oh, no! We're here!

I trail up the garden path with the others behind me. I sort of wish the path would open and swallow me up, but then I wouldn't get any presents or any cake . . .

I ring the doorbell and everyone squashes round. I can feel Cammy behind me, breathing on the back of my head.

The door swings open and there – THERE ARE FAIRY LIGHTS EVERYWHERE! The hall is all glittery and glamouroony and the weird paint spots and rainbows that Dad has painted look exotic and fridgey cool. And MY MUM! My mum is wearing the huge frilly pink and orange dress and she's put a sparkling tinsel tiara on her head!

There's a gasp from all the girls and a

big 'WOW!'

'Welcome!' 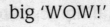 says Mum. 'Her Royal Highness Princess Glam Rock welcomes you to Fizzy Pink's Painted Party Palace!'

We all crowd into the hall and Mum shuts the door. At that moment there is a boom of drums, a twang of guitars and a tinkling of pianos as Dad leaps into the hall. He's wearing one of his shiny, sparkly Elvis outfits and he's got a karaoke microphone in his hand. I think for a moment that I might be dead embarrassed, but then he starts singing 'Blue Suede Shoes', and suddenly everyone is jumping about and singing and clapping and following Dad down the hall and all around the house.

This might not be so bad after all!

Everyone is having a totally rocking time! Even Cammy is bopping and hopping and singing along (except that she has a 'reeeely' pooey singing voice – ha, ha).

'Wow, Fizzy,' says Sally, the one who had wanted to know if I had a 'pehnie'. 'Your mum really is like a princess and your dad's amazing – I just ADORE your hise, I would simply LOVE to live in a hise like this!'

The only person who is still quiet is Daisy. I get up close to her and whisper, 'Are you OK?'

'Yes,' she says. 'It's just that everything here is so beautiful and your mum and dad's clothes and your clothes are so gorgeous that . . . well . . . oh, I don't know . . .' And then Daisy goes all sort of quiet again. She stares at the floor and starts fiddling with the holes in her jumper. Then I suddenly understand.

'I think you look really nice,' I say, because she does, and I wish I had dimples like hers, but I can tell that Daisy is feeling grottybags about what she's wearing.

'I've got an idea!' I say, very quietly, so the others don't hear. 'Come upstairs with me.' I grab her hand and we scuttle upstairs, where I stitch big sparkly flowers over the holes in her jumper, while Mum and Dad and the others carry on dancing. When

I've finished, Daisy looks so pleased and smiles so much that her dimples get ENORMOUS.

My party is FAB-BEROONY. Mum has made the biggest cake in the world in the shape of a fairy palace. She has even made little glittery fairies to put on the top and there are pink candles and letters saying 'FIZZY. TEN TODAY'.

I think everyone loves my house and my mum and dad. Everyone, that is, except for Cammy. She still looks snottybags most of the evening, but no one is taking any notice of her. The rest of us have a fantasibrill time. We play with all the things I've been given. There's a really cool game about pop stars and a sticker book with loads of stickers to put in it. I've got some pink fluffy slippers that I let everyone try on and a little toy dog that I put on my pillow. There's loads of other stuff and most of it's pink, which I LOVE.

We have a gigantic midnight feast and Cammy is the only person who is sick.

We tell each other stories all night and bounce on my bed and swap sleeping bags, and in the morning Mum makes us this HUGE breakfast. Nobody wants to eat much, but the Splat has fun splodging about in the scrambled egg and everyone thinks he's 'cute'!

When they have all gone home I give my mum and dad a big hug and thank them for the most fabberoony party EVER!

Then I go back to bed and I dream that I am a real live princess and that I live in a beautiful palace. The palace has loads of towers and right up in the highest tower I dream that I have imprisoned the evil Big Fat Fib Fairy and that she will never, ever be able to escape, ever again.

dearest darlingest Pixie

I ♡ U coz U were 🖐 ←RIGHT. 👁 told everyone about my Big Fat Fib 😠 and they all came to my party ⭐ and it was FABBEROONY (and ☹ ←sad coz U weren't there). Mum made a 🎂 ←birthday cake with 🧚 ←fairies on the top. I am sending U one of the 🧚 ←fairies. THANK YOU 4 the 🎁 ←present. I ♡ the glittery 👧 ←wig it's FAB. Miss U loads ♡ U 4 EVER — Fizzy

PS I think some of the people who came to my party might be my friends ⟶ KNOT fantasi brill like you though x x x x

♡

dearest darlingest Pixie ♡

2 day at School

u will never guess what!!!! ~~Clammy~~

Cammy ⟵ nose in the air came in2 the

🍸 glass room with ⟵ sequins stuck

on2 her ⟵ buttons!!!! Just

like ⟵ me!! She went all

⟵ sink when I said that the ⟵ buttons
P

looked glamouroony!!! Also I

have a new friend called ✳ ⟵ Daisy.

She has ⟵ ~~pimples~~ not pimples,
                    d

DIMPLES and she is nice but U

R my bestest EVER friend and I

will love u loads and always ♡

♡ X Fizzy X ♡

PS Please give your 〰 ⟵ pet snake 2

♥ ⟵ kiss from me

X X X X X X

things to make:
FLOWERS

cut out a felt flower

cut out 2 smaller felt stars in a different colour

Put them together →

and sew beads or sequins through both bits of felt (to hold the flower together)

sew a safety pin on to the back

PS If you are a real cleverclogs, you could do blanketstitch round the flower petals

blanket stitch in a different colour →

PPS If you are not such a cleverclogs, you could glue your flower together but it won't be quite as jabberoony